Throw Me Something, Mister

Story by

Malcolm Wright

Illustrated by

Meggin Davenport

Two young children see their first Mardi Gras Parade in New Orleans

AuthorHouse™
1663 Liberty Drive,
Suite 200
Bloomington, IN 47403
www.authorhouse.com
Phone: 1-800-839-8640

AuthorHouse™ UK Ltd.
500 Avebury Boulevard
Central Milton
Keynes, MK9 2BE
www.authorhouse.co.uk
Phone: 08001974150

Library of Congress Control Number: 2006902574

First published by AuthorHouse 5/24/2006

ISBN: 1-4259-2734-3 (sc)

Printed in the United States of America

Bloomington, Indiana

This book is printed on acid-free paper.

Bloomington, IN   Milton Keynes, UK

authorHOUSE

A NOTE FOR ADULTS ABOUT THIS STORY

"Throw Me Something, Mister"

This is a story about a first visit to Mardi Gras as seen through the eyes of two young children who live far from New Orleans. It was written before Hurricane Katrina devastated the city in late August of 2005 and, hopefully, presents a true picture of a more innocent and happier time. New Orleans is "The city that care forgot," a motto that needs careful understanding. It is not about indolence or unfeeling. It is about an art form of pageantry and music, of hundreds of small and large traditions woven together with such grace that recipients of these favors cannot see the effort that makes it possible for them to forget their cares for a little time in a certain place. It is about a huge, non-commercial, party called Mardi Gras given by New Orleanians to which everyone is invited, not just to stand and watch, but to participate. We hope this little book will help readers young and old understand how much will be lost if the generosity of spirit that is Mardi Gras in New Orleans is not fully restored over the next few years.

Erin and her brother Nathan were excited. Here they were in the big city of New Orleans about to see a real Mardi Gras parade. They ran up and down the "banquette" which is the old New Orleans name for sidewalk. They chased each other with the fake claws on their Mardi Gras costumes that their Maw-Maw had made for them. And they wiggled around to show off their crawfish tails. Other parents and children nearby pointed to them and laughed at the fun they were having.

All around them were the sights, sounds, and smells of the "City that Care Forgot" as New Orleans is sometimes called. Great old live oak trees arched over the streets. Spanish moss, like long gray beards, hung from their big twisting branches. Vendors in uniforms sold hotdogs from carts that looked like huge hot dogs. From sidewalk stands, you could buy rich, spicy dishes of jambalaya, crawfish pie, or red beans and rice, and soft drinks, often called "pop" in Louisiana. The clang of a trolley bell mingled with the noise of the crowd and the sad sound of a lone trumpet player a couple of blocks away.

Mardi Gras means Fat Tuesday. It is celebrated forty days before Easter in many cities around the world. The forty days before Easter are called Lent and in many Christian Churches it is a custom to make a sacrifice during Lent. This means you give up something you like very much beginning with the Wednesday after Mardi Gras until Easter Sunday. Maybe you decide not to eat candy, or watch your favorite TV programs, or maybe you promise to keep your room clean without being told to do so. The days of Lent are supposed to be a quiet, thoughtful time before Easter and Mardi Gras is often thought of as the last chance to have a lot of fun before Lent begins.

Mardi Gras in New Orleans is a huge party where everyone is invited. Every year more than a million people come to visit and see the sights. There are more than fifty parades in the ten days before Fat Tuesday. At night there are very fancy parties called balls where people wear masks and costumes like those in fairy tales. They dance to big band music. People belong to clubs called Krewes that put on the parades and balls. Many of the Krewes have strange names from Greek and Roman mythology like Rex, Orpheus, Bacchus, and Poseidon.

Erin and Nathan were from a city near the mountains where it snows in the wintertime. They and their mother, Sue, and their father, John, were visiting their grandparents in Baton Rouge, Louisiana, where the land is very flat and it almost never snows. Erin and Nathan called their grandparents Maw-Maw and Paw-Paw as many grandchildren do who live in south Louisiana.

Together they had traveled to New Orleans in Paw-Paw's big double cab pickup truck. Now they stood on St. Charles Avenue waiting for the parade of the Krewe of Rex, the king of all Mardi Gras. The kids wore the red crawfish costumes that Maw-Maw had made for them. Crawfish are important in Louisiana because many good things to eat are made from them. The local French people, who are called Cajuns, tell many funny stories and tall tales about them.

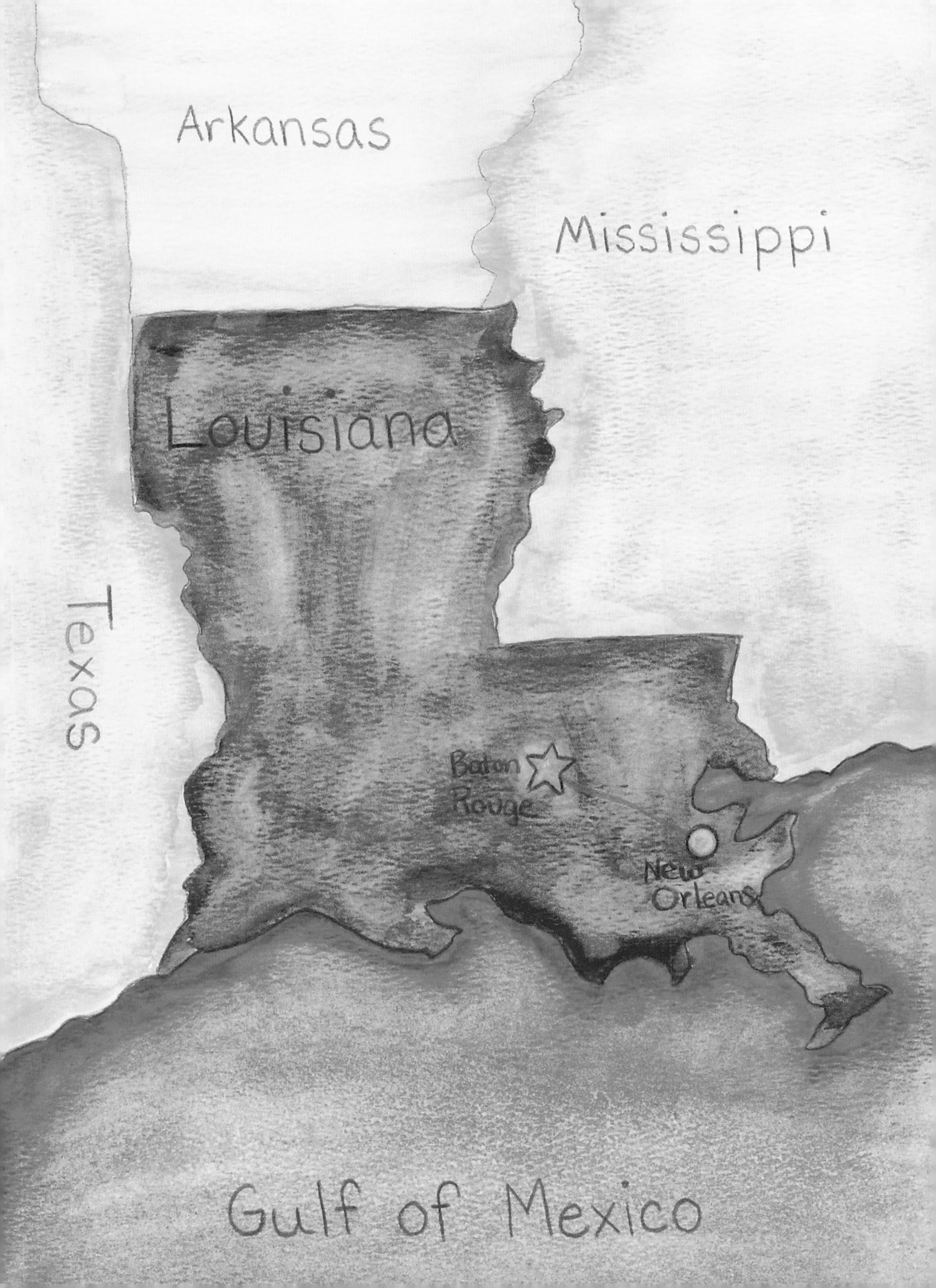
Arkansas
Mississippi
Louisiana
Texas
Baton Rouge
New Orleans
Gulf of Mexico

Paw-Paw and John put up a stepladder near the street so Erin and Nathan could sit on it to watch the parade. Paw-Paw had made a special seat on the ladder for them to sit on. It even had a seat belt so they wouldn't fall off if they got too excited. Lots of other people were doing the same thing. In fact, the street was beginning to look like a forest of ladders.

St. Charles Avenue was closed to automobile traffic for the parade. While the family waited, a big brown and green trolley rumbled down the tracks in the median of the street. Its light was on and its bell clanged to warn everyone to stand back. The trolley was crowded with people, many standing in the aisle between the seats. Erin and Nathan waved to the people inside and those near the windows waved back. It was the last trolley of the day, because trolleys, like cars, can't run during parades.

Suddenly, a band came around a corner and headed toward them. Erin and Nathan both started yelling, "Look, look. The parade is coming." But it wasn't the parade after all. It was just a single band that was having a parade by itself. The band marched - well, sort of marched - very slowly. They played a special kind of music called Dixieland Jazz, which was born in New Orleans. It had a strong beat and was kind of sweet and kind of sad all at the same time. An old black man out in front of the bandleader carried a very frilly umbrella and danced back and forth across the street. The bandleader was a big man with a goatee who played the clarinet. Every time he played a solo part, the crowd clapped and cheered. On the side of the bass drum were the words "Pete Fountain and his Half-Fast Walking Club". Mr. Pete Fountain parading with his clarinet and a group of his friends is one of many special New Orleans Mardi Gras traditions.

Lots of people were in costume - all kinds of crazy costumes. Sometimes whole families dressed alike. Many people came as Indians. Others wore native African costumes with scary masks and enormous headdresses. Erin and Nathan saw one person dressed as a unicorn, another as a lion and another as an Easter bunny. A huge Viking came by with his sword and shield, wearing a big metal hat with horns on it. Six other guys were tied together in round tubes to look like a jumbo six-pack of canned drinks with arms and legs. One kid was an astronaut, and a boy and girl were a pair of dice. A group of about ten people came by dressed as one big caterpillar. Only the face of the first one was showing and there were ten pairs of feet trying to move as one.

Twelve couples dressed in old-fashioned clown suits with tall conical hats waltzed down the street to the music of a fiddle and a small accordion playing Cajun music. Their costumes resembled those that are often worn in Mardi Gras celebrations in rural Louisiana. The crowd laughed and cheered when Nathan and Erin joined the group and tried to dance with them. Their mother (who was trying not to laugh) finally had to make them stop showing off.

"Listen, I think I hear the parade coming," said Paw-Paw. "Its almost time for you kids to get up on the ladder."

"Ooh, ooh," said Nathan looking miserable. "I have to go to the bathroom."

"Oh, I do too," said Erin.

"Oh no," said Sue looking around desperately. "What are we going to do? I don't see any bathrooms anywhere near here." John was looking in all directions, too, but there were only private homes close by. Before he could answer Maw-Maw said,

"Don't worry, I noticed some portable potties about two blocks back on a side street. Paw-Paw and I will take them there. You two stay here with our ladder." And off they went with the kids.

On the way back from the bathrooms, Nathan and Erin heard the sound of a band and the clop of horses' hooves. The parade had started while they were gone. Without thinking they grabbed each other's hands (really each other's claws) and raced toward the street before Maw-Maw or Paw-Paw could stop them. They didn't realize that the crowd had grown even bigger in the few minutes they were gone. By now the rows of people were four or five deep in front of and behind the row of stepladders. The people were jumping up and down and yelling:

"Throw me something, Mister. Throw me something, Mister," at the people who were riding on the big parade floats.

Nathan and Erin squirmed through the crowd, then under a ladder. They popped out over the curb into the street right in front of a big, fat tuba player. They had to scramble backwards to keep from getting stepped on. After the band went by, they got out in the street a little way so they could dance to its music.

"You kids better get off the street or you will be in big trouble," a deep voice rumbled from somewhere above their heads. They looked up right into the nostrils of the biggest horse they had ever seen. The rider was a New Orleans' mounted policeman, and he was shaking his nightstick at them. They squeezed back into the crowd as quickly as they could.

Almost immediately a huge float, shaped like a dragon, came along, pulled by a little tractor. It was about three times longer than Paw-Paw's pickup truck and as tall as a house. Its head and tail moved back and forth. Smoke came out of its nose every time it roared. About twenty people, all in costume, were riding on the float. They were so far up in the air on the dragon that they were above the crowd. They had necklaces of beads, doubloons and other small favors that they threw to the crowd. That is why the people in the crowd and the children on the ladders yelled, "Throw me something, Mister." When the people on the floats threw something, all of the people in the crowd jumped up and tried to catch the things before they fell to the ground.

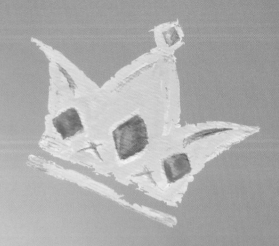

A shower of doubloons fell on Nathan and Erin just as the head of the dragon passed them. Doubloons are big coins of many colors the size of fifty-cent pieces but made of lightweight aluminum especially for Mardi Gras. The doubloons for this parade were stamped with a picture of Rex, the Mardi Gras King. A man on the float looked down and laughed and waved to them as the doubloons bounced off their heads and shoulders. Like everyone else nearby, they scrambled to pick up as many as they could before someone else got them.

Nathan and Erin were so busy collecting doubloons they didn't notice the group of rowdy teenage boys running along beside the float. The boys were not looking where they were going and ran right over the two smaller kids. Both of them were tumbled into the gutter. One of the nicer boys stopped and helped them get up. But after he had brushed them off a little and found that they were not hurt very much, he ran off to join his friends.

For the first time Nathan and Erin realized they did not know where they were. They were both dirty from falling down, Nathan had a tear in his pants on one knee and Erin's elbow was scraped. All around them were people, hundreds of people, they didn't know and who didn't know them. They were both trying not to cry. All of a sudden bands, and dragons, and horses, and doubloons, and beads were no longer much fun.

"Mom, Dad," yelled Erin.

"Maw-Maw, Paw-Paw," yelled Nathan.

But everyone was so busy yelling at the floats and catching beads that no one nearby realized the two children were lost.

"Let's go that way," said Erin, pointing in the direction the parade was coming from. "I think Momma and Daddy are down there."

Nathan couldn't think of anything else to do, so he said, "Ok, but hold my hand." Then, just as Erin was reaching for him, a big hand and arm stretched from between two ladders, grabbed Nathan and pulled him out of sight into the crowd.

Erin shouted, "Hey you, don't take my brother" and jumped toward the space where Nathan had disappeared. The hand and arm reached out again, grabbed her and she, too, was gone.

What a wonderful surprise it was when Nathan and Erin discovered that the big hand and arm that pulled them off the street actually belonged to Paw-Paw. Maw-Maw and Paw-Paw had been to many Mardi Gras parades so they knew how easily children could get lost. They had really never let them get out of sight. By the time Maw-Maw cleaned them up a little, and found them a drink of water, they were ready to see more of the parade. Before long they were seated side by side on their ladder yelling, "Throw me something, Mister" to the people riding on the floats.

It was a fantastic parade with at least thirty floats: floats that looked like frogs and alligators, floats that looked like fairy landscapes, floats like riverboats and circus merry-go-rounds. Military and high school bands from all over our country, including the United States Marine Corps Band, marched between the floats. Horses in the parade had saddles and bridles covered with silver. Some of their riders dressed as Indian Chiefs. Other riders wore elaborate western outfits and did rope tricks.

The parade lasted almost three hours. Nathan and Erin sat on their ladder and yelled, "Throw me something, Mister" until they were hoarse. The people on the floats were very generous with their beads and doubloons and small toys. Some of them had special things to throw or strings of beads longer and prettier than the regular strings. They would tease the crowd with these but would only throw one now and then.

A lady dressed as a devil on a float threw an especially long string of beads with a medallion of King Rex to Sue. But John reached in front of her and caught it. Then he laughed at Sue and teased her with it. While Sue was trying to get her beads back from John, the devil lady tossed a little doll towards them. It flew through the upraised arms of all the people that were trying to catch it and, like magic, landed right in Sue's hands. The little doll had a long black skirt, a tall black, peaked hat and a big grin on its face. Sue waved it under John's nose and said,

"You better be very careful about stealing my beads." Just as she said this a big handful of gold-colored doubloons rained down on the family.

The parade finally ended with a fire truck followed by big street sweeper trucks. Paw-Paw and John carried the ladder to the pickup and put it in the back. Then they all got in for the drive back to Baton Rouge. John, Sue and Paw-Paw sat in the front seat, Maw-Maw and the two kids in the back. Nathan and Erin went to sleep almost immediately, each clutching a huge bag full of beads, doubloons, and other things they had caught. They both dreamed of the fun they would have sharing their treasures with their friends when they got home and how they would have Mardi Gras parades in their own neighborhood and at their schools. Nathan's knee was a little sore and Erin's elbow burned a little, but those small aches just made the day seem more wonderful.

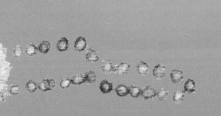
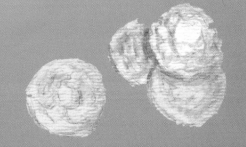

About the Author and the Illustrator

The author is a retired engineering professor who writes reminiscences and contemporary observations in short short story form, several of which have been published in a local newspaper.

The illustrator is a free lance artist who works in water colors, oils and etched glass. She also does volunteer art classes in elementary schools. She is the author's daughter.

Printed in the United States
60027LVSX00017B